CHARLIE'S SWIM

CHARLIE'S SWIM

EDITH WRIGHT
CHARMAINE LEDDEN-LEWIS

Charlie loved the smell of the ocean, creeks and clean salt air of Broome.

It reminded him of the carefree, sunny days of his childhood, going fishing and crabbing with his brothers and cousins.

As a young man, Charlie and his brother loved to run down to the foreshore to meet their father sailing into Broome. They were excited to see what he had collected from his beachcombing trip along the coast.

Charlie enjoyed
his simple life.

One day war came to Broome. Charlie did not like the smell of the planes and the fuel that wafted through the air.

Life suddenly seemed dangerous and uncertain.

During the war Charlie's job was to clean and fuel seaplanes that anchored in the bay.

The planes were carrying Dutch women and children who were being flown to safety in Australia.

One morning Charlie was working inside a seaplane. He suddenly heard planes flying overhead, they seemed incredibly low.

Charlie went outside. When he looked up he saw enemy planes swooping towards the bay.

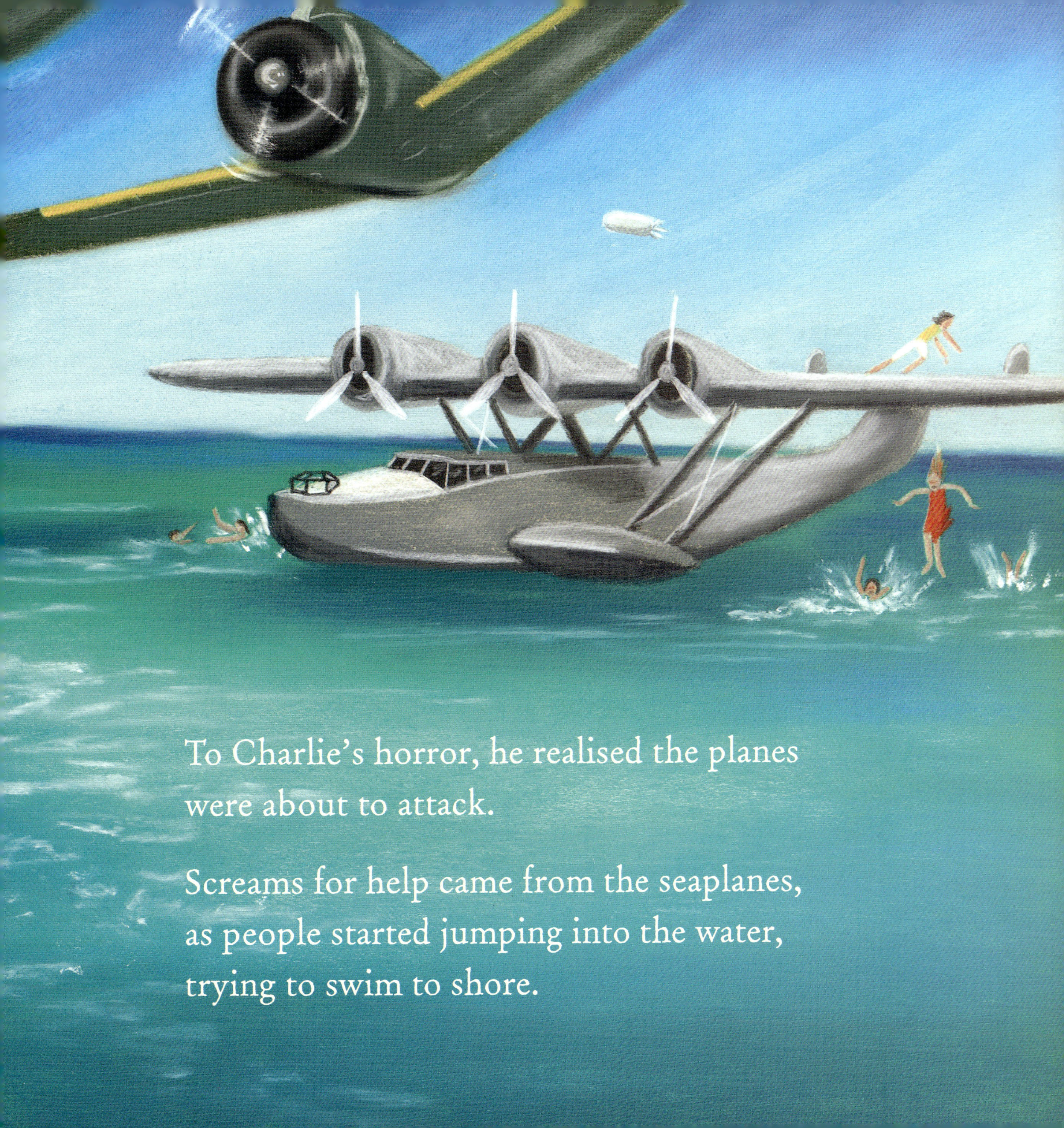

To Charlie's horror, he realised the planes were about to attack.

Screams for help came from the seaplanes, as people started jumping into the water, trying to swim to shore.

Charlie dived off the plane into the murky water. Seconds after he jumped, the plane was hit and exploded into flames.

In fear and shock, he began swimming to safety.

Charlie saw a woman and her child in distress in the water, struggling to stay afloat.

Charlie didn't think twice. He swam towards them. They were Dutch and did not speak English but he knew they needed help.

Charlie signalled for the woman and child to hold on tight to his shoulders. Luckily Charlie was a strong swimmer.

As well as watching for stray bullets, he was worried that sharks might be attracted to all the people splashing in the water.

They passed other people calling for help. Charlie felt powerless, as he could only save the woman and her child. He had to stay strong and get them to safety.

It seemed like forever before they reached the shore.

There was chaos on the beach. The sea was alight with flames from the exploding planes and the sky was black with billowing smoke.

Several boats had gone out to help the people in the water. But, sadly, not everyone could be saved. Charlie was exhausted but stayed to help.

On that sad day, more than eighty people were killed in the attack. Charlie D'Antoine was an ordinary young man who did something extraordinary.

He put his own life at risk to save a woman and her child. He was a hero but, being humble and just thankful to have survived, he never made a fuss about it.

In 1944, Charlie was awarded a Certificate of Merit from the Royal Humane Society of Australasia in recognition of his efforts, and he was awarded medals for bravery from the Dutch government.

During WWII after the Japanese invasion of Java, around 1,350 evacuees from the Dutch East Indies, many in flying boats, passed through Broome, which was a major refuelling point and a significant Allied military base. On the morning of 3 March 1942, Broome was swiftly attacked by Japanese fighter planes, killing at least 88 civilians and Allied military personnel and destroying 22 aircraft. The town and military were totally unprepared, making it the second most brutal wartime attack on Australian soil. In March the rise and fall of tides was extremely high. After the attack they had to wait until it was deep enough to get vessels into the bay.

Charlie's Swim is based on the true story of the author's Uncle Charlie (Charles D'Antoine), who was working inside a flying boat when the attack began.

In 1944, Charlie was awarded a Certificate of Merit from the Royal Humane Society of Australasia in recognition of his efforts, and he was awarded four medals for bravery from the Dutch government.

Charlie D'Antoine was a Bardi man. He was born in 1919 at Bulgin, the family homestead at the base of Hunter's Creek, a short distance from Ardiyooloon (One Arm Point Community) north of Broome. Charlie was the oldest son of Amy (Goodgie) Hunter and Richard (Ginju) D'Antoine and had five siblings. School did not feature greatly in his life and like all Aboriginal children at the time he did not go past Year 3. All his life Charlie worked hard as a labourer in the Kimberley and later worked in Darwin as a painter for the Department of Works and Housing. Upon retiring he returned to Country to enjoy fishing and reconnect with his family and Culture. Determined to make a difference for his people, he became a member of the community council, the governing body of Ardiyooloon. He held the position of Chairperson of the council for several terms. Charlie died in 1993 and was laid to rest at Ardiyooloon.

Charlie pictured in 1992 holding his Certificate of Merit and wearing one of his Dutch medals.
Courtesy Broome Historical Museum

Edith Wright (née D'Antoine) is very proud of her Bardi descent. She was born in Broome in 1954 and grew up in Derby, Western Australia. She is married with two sons and seven grandchildren. Charles D'Antoine is Edith's uncle.

In 2018 she retired from a diverse career in education which included being a teacher's assistant, classroom teacher, Principal (at Wankatjunka Remote Community School) and District Aboriginal Education Manager. All Edith's roles have focussed on addressing disadvantage and improving education outcomes for Aboriginal children and their families. Edith has published *Full Circle* which is the story of her mother and maternal grandparents. Her energy has shifted from literacy to literature. She is excited by the growing number of Aboriginal and Torres Strait Islander authors, illustrators and creators dedicating their talent and time to truth telling of the history of race relations in Australia.

Charmaine Ledden-Lewis is an award-winning illustrator and artist, and descendant of the Bundjalung people from the Clarence River, living on Dharug and Gundungurra Country in the Blue Mountains, New South Wales. Charmaine has worked with notable authors, including Bruce Pascoe and Cathy Freeman, and finds fulfilment in creating beautiful children's books by sharing stories through her art, for generations to come.